This Book Belongs To

_____

_____

_____

PLEASE LEAVE A REVIEW
BECAUSE WE WOULD LOVE TO
HEAR YOUR FEEDBACK,
OPINIONS, AND ADVICE TO
CREATE BETTER PRODUCTS
AND SERVICES FOR YOU!

YOU ARE GREATLY APPRECIATED!

THANKS FOR BEING WITH US.

SO,DON'T FORGET TO
LOOK AT OUR OTHER PRODUCTS
ON OUR AUTHOR'S PAGE.

Printed in Great Britain
by Amazon